The Witch V.I.P.

When Simon's headmaster leaves the school, the witch decides she likes the idea of being someone important and appoints herself to the job. With a little help from her magic wand she puts a spell on Mr Spigh, the school inspector sent to check up on her, but unfortunately the spell is a stale one . . .

During the school holidays the witch takes up a hobby, with disastrous results for Lady Fox-Custard, and when Simon is in hospital the witch abducts him and twenty other chidren in an ambulance. She goes on to spend a hilarious evening 'babysitting' for Simon, bodypops at the school disco and earns a fortune impersonating Guy Fawkes.

There's only one thing Simon can be sure of when the witch is around – there'll be trouble!

The Witch V.I.P.

Margaret Stuart Barry

Illustrated by Linda Birch

Young Lions

First published in Great Britain 1987 by William Collins Sons & Co. Ltd
First published in Young Lions 1988
Second impression October 1988

Young Lions is an imprint of
the Children's Division, part of
the Collins Publishing Group,
8 Grafton Street, London W1X 3LA

Text copyright © 1987 by Margaret Stuart Barry
Illustrations copyright © 1987 by Linda Birch

Printed and bound in Great Britain by
William Collins Sons & Co. Ltd, Glasgow

Contents

To Nick and Rosie Bate

The Witch
and the Stale Spell

Simon was on his way to see his friend, the witch. He was so excited his legs couldn't seem to catch up with the top of him and his face was so pink it clashed with his jersey.

"Guess what!" he exploded, as he landed on the witch's doorstep.

"You're training to win the ten thousand mile race in the Olympics," guessed the witch.

"No," said Simon.

"You're going to a fancy dress party and you're pretending to be a lobster," guessed the witch again.

"No," puffed Simon, " – Mr Bodley, the headmaster, has left!"

The witch looked disappointed and went back to her housework which was stamping on beetles and scooping them up into jam jars for future beetle pies.

"But you don't understand," Simon went on, "that means we'll be getting a *new* head teacher."

The witch, who had never liked the old one much — on account of him never liking *her*, thought it was very tiresome to have to start getting used to another rotten head, and decided she would take the job herself. She fancied being someone important.

"But you can't do that!" gasped Simon, turning from a lobster into a lily, "you've got to be a proper teacher."

"Teachers only sit down all day and say things like, 'read this' and 'read that' and 'add that up' and 'take this away', and go round shouting and banging desk lids. *I* could do that."

Simon couldn't think what else to say. He'd never actually *seen* Mr Bodley doing any work. It did seem to be a jolly easy job. But what would all the parents think if the new head teacher turned out to be a witch?

As it happened, none of his friends, not even his own mother, would ever believe that the witch really *was* a witch.

"She's just a scruffy old woman," snorted Sally, who was on reading book one hundred and ninety and very stuck up.

Next morning, Sally's mother was at the school gate, chatting to Simon's mother.

"I must say," she was saying, "she's a queer

looking headmistress, she's got soup stains all down herself."

"But she's quite a kind old lady," said Simon's mother, vaguely. "I expect she's just minding the place, or something."

Meanwhile, the witch was getting used to what head teachers do. She was sitting on a comfy chair and having a cup of tea.

"It's pouring!" complained Sally. "That old bat should open the door and let us in."

But the witch had just discovered that the chair whizzed round and round.

It began to bucket down outside, but the chair was going faster and faster and the witch was getting dizzier and dizzier. Suddenly, she flew off and shot straight through the window and landed in the playground.

"Get inside, you silly children!" yelled the witch, pretending that she'd come out of the window on purpose.

Soaking wet, the children sat on the hall floor and waited to hear what next.

"Your headmaster, Mr Bodley, has gone and left," said the witch. "He got sick. Sick of *you*!" She rolled around the stage, laughing at her own joke. "And we were sick of *him*!" she choked.

Some of the braver children laughed too. Jimmy Watson laughed very loudly, but it was more in terror than anything.

"So, I'm headmistress now."

"I bet they won't let her be," whispered Sally.

"Letter 'b'?" asked the witch, who had ears that could pick up the sound of a flea sneezing. "Letter 'b' is for 'beetles', 'bugs' and 'busy bodies'."

Sally went very red.

Simon was still worried about the witch making herself head. He liked it of course, but he was afraid that there was sure to be trouble. Enjoying herself hugely, the witch burst into the staff room. The teachers were waiting for the bell to go and hoping it wouldn't.

"Right," greeted the witch, "who teaches sums?"

"I do," said Mr Diddle, importantly.

"Well you can push off," said the witch.

"D'you mean you've given me the sack?" gasped Mr Diddle.

The witch thought he was potty – seeing sacks that weren't there, but she said, "Yes, and you can stuff all your nasty hard sums in it and take them home with you. Now, who teaches history?"

"I do," said Miss Stuffy.

"Well you can have a sack too," said the witch. "We'd rather have lolly ices than old dates."

Miss Grunt, who taught reading, and was therefore Sally's favourite started to grumble.

"And *you* can go too," the witch told her. "We don't want any more of 'the cat sat on the mat', 'the fat rat sat on the cat' business."

Miss Grunt was furious. She squashed on her big hat and stamped off, grunting that she was going to report the witch to *someone*.

There was only Miss Phoeble left.

"She's a wonderful pencil sharpener," said the witch, and told her to sharpen some and then give out the comics.

"Gosh!" said Jimmy Watson when he found out that all the teachers had left except Miss Phoeble, "I hope she hasn't sacked the dinner-lady too. It would be really terrible if the dinner-lady went."

"Is that all you can think about?" scoffed Sally. "That old woman can't just walk in here and make herself headmistress and throw out all the teachers without getting into big trouble."

"Take that girl's comic off her," snapped the

witch, "and give her a hard spelling book."

But Sally loved hard spelling books and went off to enjoy it. But Simon went on worrying. The witch was the most un-boring person he knew. She did things other people would never dare to do, or even think of doing. Mostly, they were funny, but sometimes they seemed dangerous. She was still playing whizzies in the headmaster's chair.

"That's awfully dangerous," exclaimed Simon.

"I know," giggled the witch, "I've already been shot through the window six times."

"I didn't mean the chair," scolded Simon, "I meant making yourself headmistress. One can't do that sort of thing."

"But I just did it," said the witch, flying off and landing in the typewriter.

"They might send you to prison," warned Simon.

"Don't be such a boring old spoilsport," laughed the witch, and hopped off to see the dinner-lady.

The dinner-lady was putting on her pinny.

"Is it ready yet?" the witch asked her.

"Of course not," said the dinner-lady, "it's only ten thirty."

"In future, lunch will be two hours early every day," said the witch.

"Who says so?"

"I says so," said the witch, "and I'm the new headmistress."

"And I'm the Queen Mum," said the dinner-lady.

"Oh," said the witch, "well tomorrow we want it early anyway. I can see why being a headmistress is difficult," the witch said to Simon, "even the Queen Mum won't do as she's told."

All this time, Miss Grunt had been down town — complaining about the witch. At first, no one would believe her. They thought she'd gone mad, like some teachers do. But, just in case, they sent Mr Spigh, a school inspector. When Sally caught sight of him, coming across the playground in his striped trousers, black hat, and sharpened umbrella, she was very gleeful. At last there was going to be trouble for the witch.

The witch was standing on top of the dining hall table with a large pan of peas and shouting, "Anyone for seconds?"

"Me please," squeaked Jimmy Watson in horrified delight as the witch peppered him with peas from a vast distance.

Most of the peas missed Jimmy Watson by a mile and struck the school inspector.

"I want a word with you in the headmaster's office," said Mr Spigh.

"Headmistress's," corrected the witch, giving the children a half day off and disappearing into her room.

The witch found the school inspector hard to talk

to, he kept shouting at her and pointing his finger like a dagger. He went on and on. Suddenly, the witch remembered her Magic Spell book and looked up, 's' for sticky, 's' for smelly, 's' for stuffy, and 's' for statue. Hastily, she pointed her wand under the inspector's nose and gabbled,

> "Silly sausage, Mr Spigh,
> snoopy snoppy one black eye,
> turn into a STATUE."

Immediately, Mr Spigh began to go stiff; another wiggle of the witch's wand and he turned into a statue, his umbrella raised over his head like a javelin.

"Hurray!" squawked the witch: not all her spells worked first time. She shoved him into the corridor and went home.

Next day, all the children arrived early. They were looking forward to reading more comics and the witch was looking forward to being headmistress again.

"Go and fetch the registers," she said, bossily, to Jimmy Watson. Jimmy Watson went and came back again in one second.

"I can't," he trembled, whiter than a piece of chalk, "there's a big black monster sitting on them."

"Monster? What does this monster look like?" the witch asked.

"It's got dirty black fluff, all stuck together and full of fleas. S'got one and a half ears, and one of its eyes is green and the other one's yellow, and its claws are going in and out of its paws."

"Pah!" scoffed the witch, "that's only George, me cat; just shove him off."

"I can't," wailed Jimmy Watson, "it was getting ready to spring at me."

"Oh rubbish!" said the witch. "I'll get the registers myself."

But George, who never got properly fed at home – on account of the witch always forgetting, had just finished eating the last one. Before the witch could

smack him, he had sprung up onto the top of the
blackboard where he slunk, picking his teeth and
spitting down left over bits of children's names.

"Disgusting animal!" shuddered Sally.

"We're going to have a Parents' Evening," announced the witch. "Tick your own sums right,
throw all your bad work in the bins, and draw some
pictures for the walls."

"I haven't got any bad work," snooted Sally.

"None at all?" asked the witch, standing by
mistake on Sally's writing book.

It was then that Sally noticed Mr Spigh standing in
the corridor. "What on earth . . . !?"

"Oh gosh!" gasped Simon, "that's er . . . um . . .
wotsit."

"That's Mr Spigh," shouted Sally.

"That's the Patron Saint of our school, it's Saint Edmund," the witch said, booming up out of nowhere, the way she often did.

By now, all the children were crowding round Mr Spigh, peering at him and touching him.

"It's Mr SPIGH!" insisted Sally. "*She's* done something to him."

"Patron Saint," said the witch.

"It isn't!" yelled Sally.

"I thought patron saints wore nighties, and things," whispered Jimmy Watson.

"Only the old fashioned ones," informed the witch, who had nothing more to say except that the parents would be arriving any minute. And she went out into the playground with a piece of chalk and wrote on the wall, as big as she could,

THE WITCH RULES, O.K.

The parents had thought that their children had just been babbling on when they'd said that a witch had made herself headmistress. They hadn't believed that all the teachers had left and that the only lessons were comics and drawing and dinnertime.

"Good evening all," the witch was saying, "hang your coats on the floor, the Queen Mum is serving coffee."

Our Nature finds!

Sally's mother swiftly put on a posh face and took it off again when she saw it was only the dinner-lady.

The parents didn't bother to look at any of the art but dashed straight for the sum books. They were delighted to find so many ticks until Mr Watson said, "Jimmy – you've ticked five and five make twelve."

Jimmy looked half pleased and half worried.

"She told us to tick them," said Sally. "I'm the only one who's *really* got them all right."

Just then, the parents noticed Mr Spigh standing in the corridor.

"Saint Edmund," explained the witch.

"Fibber!" said Sally.

"Darling!" exclaimed her mother.

"But it's a school inspector," shrieked Sally, "can't you all *see*? She's DONE something to him."

The witch wanted to do something to Sally but she couldn't with so many parents around, so she kept up her headmistress toothy grin.

Mr Spigh had been a statue for two days now and he was absolutely furious, but he couldn't move a muscle. He could however make his face go purple with rage.

"Ooh look!" squealed Jimmy Watson, tugging at his father's coat in terror, "the statue's going purple!"

"Oh they often do that; go purple and things," explained the witch, "it's hard being a saint."

But the parents were getting more and more

suspicious about the purple-faced saint who was wearing a black suit and a bowler hat and looked exactly like a school inspector, and they began to prod him.

"Drat!" muttered the witch to herself. "I must've used a stale spell. The pesky thing's starting to wear off."

The witch wished she could turn all the nosey parents into beetles, then she would be able to sweep them up and throw them out of the window. But she knew if she did that there would be more trouble, and Simon, who was her best friend, might not like his mother being a beetle.

21

"There are more lovely refreshments in the hall," she shouted, skipping off in a jolly isn't-this-tremendous-fun sort of way.

But nobody followed her, they were all crowded round Mr Spigh, watching him get twitchier and twitchier.

"I'm going to sing a song – and do some aerobics," trilled the witch, but the parents were watching Mr Spigh getting wobblier and wobblier.

"I'm going to climb Everest and jump off the top and knit a pair of socks on the way down," the witch hooted, but the parents were watching Mr Spigh opening his eyes.

"Good gracious!" exclaimed the witch. "What a funny thing to happen! Fancy a snoopy old school inspector playing such a smashing trick and pretending to be a statue. It had *me* fooled! Well done Mr Sooper Snoop!"

"Spigh," corrected the inspector.

"Sooper Spy," agreed the witch.

Then everyone began to laugh and thought what a good sport Mr Spigh seemed to be, and what a jolly old lady the witch was. Mr Spigh didn't feel like a good sport, he felt stiff and savage, but he could see the tip of the witch's wand sticking out of her handbag, so he squeezed out a pretend laugh and went home.

The Disastrous Hobby

The next day when the witch went to school, there was nobody there. Not even the Queen Mum had turned up.

"What a lazy lot of little skippers!" exclaimed the witch. Anyway, the witch decided she needed a rest because teaching was exhausting – even with all those long holidays. She set off to town for a coffee and bumped into Simon who was doing nothing.

"Hey! You saucy little skipper!" she greeted him. "Why aren't you at school today?"

"Because it's the summer holiday," Simon told her.

"Already?" gasped the witch. "I never know what to do on a holiday."

Simon looked puzzled. As far as he could see, the witch was always on holiday.

"What do you do on a holiday?" the witch asked him.

"Well," laughed Simon, "I play with my friends; sometimes I go to the seaside, and I do my hobbies."

The witch thought doing hobbies sounded interesting. "How do you do a hobby?" she asked.

Simon tried to explain about hobbies. "Well my hobby is collecting old stamps," he started.

"What use are *old* ones?" asked the witch. "D'you put glue on 'em and use them again?"

"Gosh no!" said Simon, "I just keep them in an album and er . . . look at them."

"Cripes!" said the witch. "How boring. Think of one for me."

"I know," said Simon, "we could go to the library and find one from a book."

"Well let's hurry then before I get bored stiff," cried the witch.

At the sight of so many books, the witch nearly ran away. "Heck!" she said.

"Ssh," said the librarian.

"Sssh," said Simon.

"Ssssh," said the witch. "Sssh, sssh, sssh, ssssssh."

"Ssh," said the librarian again.

"Is that woman potty?" the witch asked Simon, " – she keeps making noises like a steam engine."

"You're supposed to talk quietly in a library, that's why," Simon explained.

"Oh," said the witch.

They found a book about hobbies and sat down to read it. It started –

'a' for aeroplane making.
'b' for budgie breeding.
'c' for custard pie throwing.
'd' for diamond mining.
'e' for elephant stuffing.

"Golly!" exploded Simon.

"I was only joking," tittered the witch.

"Ssh," said the librarian.

> 'f' for fishing.
> 'g' for garden gnomes.
> 'h' for house repairs.

"Yuck!" said Simon.

"*That's* what I want to do," decided the witch. "Let's hurry."

"Hey you!" shouted the librarian, quietly, "you haven't had that book stamped."

"Oh, sorry Mrs Shush," said the witch. "I didn't know books had to be stamped on. I'll do it."

She put the book on the floor and stamped on it with both feet.

Looking at the outside of the witch's house, Simon could see why the witch wanted to learn about house repairs. The nasturtiums which grew among the cabbages had now grown so wild they had reached the chimney and were beginning to grow down inside it.

"I think I'll wallpaper first," said the witch. "It looks jolly easy." She pasted up some black paper and blobbed silver stars on it. Then she painted rainbows all over the ceiling, the fireplace, and the television. The rug, on which George glued himself most days, was so muddy, the witch threw grass seed on it.

"S'good isn't it?" she grinned when she had finished. "I didn't know the place could look so different."

Simon wasn't sure. "It's different," he mumbled.

"EXACTLY," said the witch. "And that's what people want isn't it? I think this hobby is a smashing one because I can make a lot of money out of it as well."

She painted a board and stuck it in her hedge. It said:

•MAKE YOUR HOUSE DIFFRUNT.

•HAVE iT PAINTUD. AND.

•MENDUD BY ME...

"Oh no!" groaned Simon. "If you don't mind, I'll just go home and stick some stamps in my album."

"O.K." said the witch, "I'm going to be busy now anyway."

But she wasn't. People stopped to read her notice; looked at the house; shuddered, and walked on again.

"Probably they think it's going to be too dear," thought the witch, and she wrote another bit on the bottom of her sign which said:

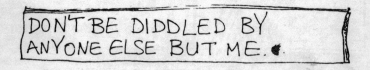

DON'T BE DIDDLED BY
ANYONE ELSE BUT ME.

Simon kept out of the witch's way for a week after

that. He went fishing with Jimmy Watson, agreed to have tea at Sally's house because his mother and her mother wanted him to, and then his curiosity got the better of him and he went to see the witch. He looked nervously at the other houses in her road, but to his relief, they all looked the same as usual. He found the witch mowing her hearthrug.

"Been busy have you?" Simon asked.

"No," snapped the witch, stamping on a dandelion.

"I'm sorry," said Simon.

"You look it," said the witch.

"If I were you," Simon went on nervously, "I'd choose a different hobby."

"I like this one," sulked the witch. "If people knew how clever I am they'd be queueing up to get me."

A glint came into her eye, and Simon knew his friend had just had one of her terrible ideas. "I'll ring up Lady Fox-Custard," she was saying, "then people will see how important I am, when they see what I've done to her house."

"Hullo," said the gardener, "her Ladyship's on holiday."

"I know," lied the witch. "That's why I'm going to start painting and mending her house tomorrow."

"She never told me," grumbled the gardener.

"Course she didn't, I'm doing it as a surprise. I'm a

29

famous decorator."

"I see," said the gardener.

"I think this is the worst idea you've ever had," puffed Simon, as he helped the witch to carry her ladder the next day.

"You don't need to come," said the witch.

But Simon thought he'd better. Maybe he could still make the witch change her mind.

Lady Fox-Custard's house was the biggest in the town. It had fancy turrets, and flag poles, and lily ponds, and twiddley railings, and two stone lions sitting on the gate posts. Simon's mother called it vulgar, but not so's Lady Fox-Custard could hear her.

"She never told me nuffink," the gardener was still grumbling when they arrived.

"Go and dig yer spuds," the witch said.

"Eeeh!" said Simon, as the witch crashed the ladder up against the front of the house.

"I don't think those bumpy bits on the roof look good," she said.

"They're the turrets!" squealed Simon.

"Got to go," said the witch, as she got to work with a hammer. She stood back to look at her handiwork.

"That's smoother looking," she said, "they were going up and down and up and down and up and down. And, heck: I don't think Custard should hang her washing on the roof!" and she cut the flag down and put it on the gardener's bonfire.

"Now the inside," she said. "What do you think?"

"I think we should go home," gasped Simon.

"With the job only half done!?" cried the witch. "We've got to give Fox-Custard a really BIG surprise. I must think arty crafty."

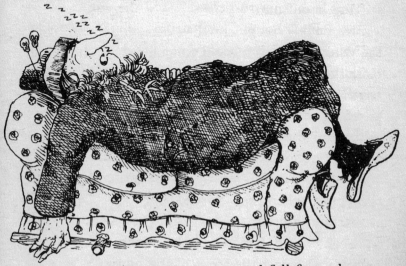

She flung herself on the settee and fell fast asleep – dreaming, and puffing little snores up into her hat. Simon was just about to creep away when the witch sat up suddenly, looking very bright.

"I'm going to paint wonderful ghosts all over the house – 'cos it's the sort of house that should have lots of ghosts, and skeletons, and creepy crawlies."

"She'll HATE it!" Simon begged the witch not to bother.

"S'no bother," beamed the witch. "Mix that paint sludgy grey for me."

She started to zoom round the room with her paintbrush. She painted fat ghosts and skinny ghosts. Ghosts sitting on the mantlepiece and ghosts climbing up the stairs. There were ghosts in the bathroom, brushing their teeth, and ghosts in the kitchen, stirring bone soup.

"Now a few creepy crawlies, here, and there," said the witch, sticking out her tongue so that she could paint them carefully, "and it's finished. Gosh! It looks terrific! I'll be famous after this." She left a note on the table:

YOO OWE ME ONE HUNDRUD POUNDS
HOP YOO LIKIT.

Lady Fox-Custard had been to London to see the Queen. And she'd seen her through the railings. She was going to have a tea party when she got back home and tell all her friends how wonderful it had been, and how she'd chatted to the Queen for hours and hours. There was no need to tell them that she'd shouted, 'We love you, Your Majesty', and that the Queen hadn't actually heard her. She would have tiny cucumber sandwiches, and meringues, and red, white and blue jellies. She drove her car into her drive and then out again.

"Silly me!" she said, "I thought that was my house." Then to her horror and dreadful shock, she found that it *was* her house.

"What's happened to me turrets!?" she screamed, "and me flag!?"

The gardener came hobbling up. "I thought you'd be surprised," he said. "This old woman's been and decorated. She's done you all over."

Lady Fox-Custard stumbled inside the house and promptly fainted. The doctor came and said, "My goodness! You look as if you've seen a ghost!" and gave her some medicine to take.

When Lady Fox-Custard was well enough, she drove down to the witch's house in a terrible temper.

"Ah," said the witch. "Have you come to pay me? Did you love it? And are you going to tell all your friends how terrific it is?"

Lady Fox-Custard sputtered like a porpoise, and sticking her nose over the witch's gate, she bellowed, "I am NOT going to pay you, and I do NOT love it, and I am NOT going to go round the town and tell my friends how terrific it is. I am going to tell everyone what a dreadful mess you have made of my lovely house; what a ROTTEN decorator you are, and that you are a wicked, wicked vandal!"

"Golly!" said the witch, "some people are never pleased." And she took the hobbies book back to the library.

"Here, Mrs Shush," she said, "*You* can stamp on my book this time. It's rotten!"

Fantastic Doctor No-all

It was mizzleing as Simon set off to the river with Jimmy Watson.

"When it mizzles like this," he was saying, "the fish really start jumping. They love it."

"They won't love it when we start catching them," Jimmy smiled at the thought.

"I should have asked the witch to come really," Simon went on. "She's fresh out of hobbies. But she'd probably flump along the bank like a great black bat and make a noise, and that's no good for fishing."

"No," agreed Jimmy, jolly glad that the witch wasn't coming.

The fish were jumping. They looked as if they were trying to catch the raindrops with their mouths. Simon and Jimmy thrashed away excitedly with their rods for about an hour, but they caught nothing –

except a string of weed and a tree behind them. Then they ate their sandwiches and thought how interesting it all was.

"She'd be bored," said Simon. "Too slow for her."

"She'd throw a stick of dynamite in the river and BLOW them out!" giggled Jimmy. "There'd be fish for a thousand miles around. Right up the bank anyway."

They decided to have one more try and then go home. Simon flung his line into the very middle of the river, and his rod bent double.

"I've GOT one!" he screamed. "It feels like a whale!"

"I'll help you," shouted Jimmy, crashing into Simon, who tripped and stuck his leg down a sandy hole. "Ow! I've broken my leg!" he howled.

"Have you lost the whale?"

"Course, and I've lost my rod," wailed Simon, " – but I've got a BROKEN LEG! Twit!"

"Oh," said Jimmy, who never knew what to do when he was in the middle of a tragedy.

"You could try pulling me out," snapped Simon.

Jimmy managed to pull Simon a bit further up the bank, and then he ran off.

His legs seemed to have shrunk as he fled across the field towards the road. Speechless, he arrived at Simon's house.

"Yes, Jimmy?" Simon's mother said.

Jimmy carried on being speechless. When his chest had stopped going in and out like a worn-out pair of bellows, he gasped, "Your Simon's broke his leg trying to land a whale."

"Start again," asked Simon's mother.

"Simon's broken a whale trying to land his leg."

Simon lay on the bank, wondering why Jimmy had taken fright when he most needed him. If the witch had come with them, she could have magicked up a stretcher, or better still, an ambulance. He was just in the middle of this happy thought, when to his surprise, an ambulance did come wobbling across the field. In it were his mother and Jimmy Watson.

"I think he's broken his leg all right," said the ambulance man as he tied it up.

"What a good job you're on holiday," said his mother, unhelpfully.

One good thing about the hospital – they were just serving the tea.

"If you're not well, I'll eat your jam," obliged a small girl in the bed next to him, who had so many freckles over her she looked as if she had incurable ginger measles. "And after I've eaten it, I'll sign your leg for you."

She drew pigs on his plaster and the other children queued up to draw their things.

"Into bed," shouted Sister, "or I won't let the

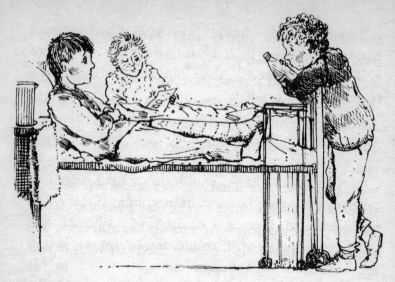

visitors in."

Jimmy Watson came down the ward, struggling with two bottles of orange juice and a big bag of lemon sherberts.

"Are you feeling better?" he asked.

"I've only just got here," said Simon. "Are those for me?"

"Yes," said Jimmy, starting a lemon sherbert himself to see if they were all right. "That's a weird looking girl next to you."

"She's good at drawing pigs," Simon said. "She pinched my jam at teatime."

"I found your rod in the river. It was snapped in half, but my dad's super-glued it."

There was a kerfuffle at the end of the ward.

"There's a trampess in the corridor," informed

38

Freckles. "Sister Blister will probably ring the police."

The witch had arrived. She was wearing what she thought of as her best dress. That is to say, it had fewer soup stains down the front of it than her usual one. Her hat was tied to her collar with a shoe lace, because that too was her visiting hat and she didn't want to lose it. Her handbag was half-open because she'd bought some chips on the way over and hadn't had time to finish them. And under her other arm was squashed George, his mouth puffed out with mouse fur.

"Is it or is it not visiting time?" the witch was booming.

Sister Blister was a pretty good boomer herself and she had taken a hearty dislike to the witch. She looked at the witch's clothes and thought to herself that she was sure to be bringing a whole new lot of unknown germs into the ward. Her white frilly hat shook, indignantly, on the top of her head.

"There's something funny on the top of your head!" cried the witch, suddenly.

"What?" gasped the sister, feeling quickly. "What is it?"

"Dunno," said the witch. "It looks like a squashed meringue."

At that moment, a nurse called to say there was a phone call for Sister Blister, and the witch shot smartly into the ward.

Simon was delighted to see her.

"That Sister Blister's a head case!" the witch said, refreshing herself with some of Simon's sherberts and washing them down with a lot of orange juice. "She weren't going to let me in – just because I don't look like all the other dowdy mothers. I shouldn't have bothered dressing up."

"Aren't you a trampess then?" asked Freckles, who was now out of bed and examining the witch with admiration.

The witch adored being admired and started to

40

show off. She stood on her head and whistled three verses of, 'Yes, we have no bananas'.

"What big knickers!" giggled Freckles.

By now, all the children were out of their own beds and sitting on Simon's. A little nurse came down and said, "Sorry, I want to take their temperatures now."

"You needn't bother," said the witch, "I can tell you now, it's going to be showers with sunny spells."

The nurse went away tittering and the medicine trolley came round, rattling with bottles and pills.

"I'll have a coke please, and a box of those smarties," said the witch.

The children screamed with laughter, and one of the little boys, who had his leg in plaster, the same as Simon's, fell off the bed and rolled around the floor, laughing louder than ever.

The witch was beside herself with so much interest being taken in her and started to do a trapeze act, walking along the childrens' bed rails and leaping from one bed to another. With each leap, she shot up her umbrella to act as a parachute.

"Hey! Look at that disgusting looking cat!" squealed a spotty looking boy called Guy. "It's been eating mice!"

George, who was half bounced out of the witch's pocket, gave Guy a slit-eyed glare and leapt into his locker, to see if there were mice in there. He found nothing but a bag of crisps. He scattered those on the floor and munched up the shiny bag. Then he sprang into the witch's handbag for a cat nap.

"That fleabitten cat's a thief!" yelled Guy, furiously.

"Well you shouldn't've made personal remarks about him," was all the witch said. "Let's play Jumping Monkeys!"

"How do you play Jumping Monkeys?" squealed Freckles, who couldn't wait to learn the rules.

"Well if you've got a broken leg," explained the witch, "you can't play at all. But if you've got two ordinary legs, you stand on one bed, like this, and you jump across the floor to the next bed. And if you get good at it, you stand on the first bed and jump onto number three bed. And if you get monkier than that, you stand on the first bed and jump all the way to the fourth bed, and the monkey that can jump over the most beds is the winner."

"And if you miss and fall inbetween then you get killed I suppose," said Simon, beginning to think the witch's ideas were getting too silly.

"Nobody'll get killed," scoffed the witch. "We'll put all the pillows on the floor."

All the children queued to play monkeys. Spotty

43

Guy, who was in a good mood again, jumped two beds. Jimmy Watson managed four. Several of the children missed altogether and landed on the floor, but the pillows were bouncy enough to stop them getting hurt. Then Freckles, who looked a bit like a monkey anyway, did six.

"I bet I've won!" she squealed. "I've done SIX! Nobody can beat that."

"I haven't had my turn yet though," said the witch. And she stood on bed number one and shot off like a rocket into space. As she flew through the air, she looked like a large bat. She landed at the very bottom end of the ward on bed twenty.

"Hip hip . . . hooray!" she yelled. "Y'can't beat that, unless you do a boomerang and come back the other side. I'm the biggest monkey in the world! O.K."

The children all cheered very loudly, except Freckles who felt the witch must have some kind of electric catapult hidden in her knickers.

"She's a witch, you see," explained Simon.

"You're telling me!" agreed Freckles.

Before the witch could ask what the prize was going to be, Sister Blister came charging onto the ward, popping with fury. "Get out, you!" she bellowed at the witch.

"Visiting time's not over is it?" said the witch.

"It is for you."

"Gosh!" said the witch. "I was only trying to cheer 'em up. They were looking pretty jolly bored." She collected her handbag and muttered to Simon, "I bet you wish you could get out of this place."

"Course," said Simon, "everybody'd like to get out of hospital."

Sitting at home, munching her beetle sandwiches, the witch decided she must rescue Simon. 'Everybody wanted to get out of hospital' he'd said. Next visiting time, she arrived early at the ward.

"OUT!" said Sister Blister.

The witch went home and thoughtfully stirred up some spider soup. It was obvious the sister remembered her and she wasn't going to let her through the door. She arrived at the hospital again, and tucking her skirt in her knickers, and putting George safely under her hat, she started to climb up the drainpipe.

She had only just got her nose safely over the windowsill when Sister Blister spotted her.

"OUT, I said!" she shouted.

The witch landed heavily in the carpark. Home yet again, and spreading caterpillar sauce onto a banana, the witch screwed up her brain really hard to make it think of a good idea. And she had one.

She got out her magic spell book and looked up 'd' for duck, 'd' for dirty doormat, 'd' for dustbin, and 'd' for doctor. Waving her wand round herself, she said,

"Nurses and sisters
and nasty old blisters,
Hospital puddings that go pop in your tummy —
Make me a doctor wot looks 'portant — not funny."

She looked in the mirror and was really pleased at what she saw.

She was in a long white coat which had pockets full of pens and silver things which looked like scissors, but weren't. Out of one pocket hung another silver gadget with rubber tubes on it, for listening into people's chests to see if they had hearts, or not. And on her chest was a badge which said, 'Doctor No-All'.

This time, she walked through the hospital front door. The other doctors were walking around slowly, with their hands behind their backs. So the witch did the same.

Sister Blister was drinking a cup of tea, which she quickly threw down the sink.

"Good morning Doctor," she said, patting the meringue on the top of her head and trying to look pretty.

"Good morning, Sister Blister," said the witch in a gruff voice. "I want to examine all the children this morning."

"Back into bed everybody," clapped Sister. "Doctor's coming round to see you."

"This is great!" thought the witch as she went from bed to bed, listening to chests with her stethescope and wondering if she was doing it right.

"What can you hear in my chest?" asked Freckles.

"Top of the pops," said the witch.

Freckles giggled loudly and Sister Blister gave her a puzzled look.

"What can you hear in MY chest?" Simon asked.

"The nine o'clock news," said the witch.

"You're the WITCH!" gasped Simon.

"Shush!" she said.

Quiet giggles went all round the ward.

"We've never seen *her* before," whispered Spotty Guy. "She's a bit funny peculiar."

"Right, Sister Blister," said the witch when she had finished her round. "I want all this lot down to X-ray."

"ALL of them!?" gasped the sister.

"I'll examine your ears later," added the witch. "Now get some wheelchairs for the daft ones wot've broken their legs etcetera, and look sharp."

"Yes, Doctor No-All," said Sister Blister, not daring to disobey, but secretly hopping mad.

All the children hopped and limped and wheeled themselves towards the lift.

"Squash in," shouted the witch. "Going down . . . pots and pans . . . videos and tellys . . . ladies underwear . . . groundfloor – shift along please to the front entrance."

"But I thought we were going to X-ray?" said Freckles.

"Who'd want a photo of you!" joked the witch, beginning to hurry as she noticed other doctors giving her odd looks.

Just as she'd hoped, there was an empty ambulance parked outside. She squashed the children into the back of it, leapt into the driving seat and shot off.

"I hope I know how to drive this thing," she remarked after they'd gone ten miles at a speed faster than sound. The blue light was twirling round on the roof and the siren was going, *wee ooh wee ooh wee ooh*. The witch felt drunk with pleasure.

"What's happening to us?" asked Spotty Guy.

"Oh, didn't I tell you?" said the witch. "You're being rescued. *Everybody* wants to get out of hospital, don't they?"

Suddenly, she slammed on the brakes. They had arrived outside Mr Valdini's cafe.

Mr Valdini stood with his mouth open as the children wobbled in and flopped down. He thought perhaps a new war had started.

"Have you never seen people being rescued before?" snapped the witch. "We'll have twenty ice creams with chocolate flakes, pistachio nuts, and cherries on top. And don't be stingey with the strawberry squirt thingummy."

Alarmed at the sight of such an important looking doctor in his cafe, Mr Valdini hurried to make the ices.

"Gosh, what fun!" squeaked Freckles, ecstatically. "I wonder what Sister Blister would say?"

The witch tittered. "She'd say:

Doctor No-All's a very good doctor,
her medicine is ice cream and nuts.
She's famous and clever,
and never says never,
so no shan'ts and no can'ts and no buts."

"That's not a very good poem," laughed Simon.

"Well poetry's jolly hard," sulked the witch. "You make up a better one, pot leg."

All this time, Mr Valdini was staring at the witch, and he could have sworn that he saw a scruffy black head sticking out of her overall pocket. Perhaps it was a hot water bottle cover . . . or something. Then, as the witch chattered on merrily about famous oper-

50

ations she'd done, and how she'd once driven an ambulance up to the top of Everest to give an aspirin to a climber who had a headache – the strangest thing began to happen to her white coat. The children gaped as small black patches began to appear on it. They grew bigger and bigger, until in the end, the witch was back in her old dress. Her grey hair, which looked like the stuffing out of an old cushion, had straggled down onto her shoulders, and her face had returned to its usual greenish colour. George, who felt he'd been squashed in the witch's pocket long enough, sprang on to the counter and sneezed violently all over Mr Valdini's cakes. The children were shocked and delighted.

"I *thought* you were a funny-looking sort of doctor," said Spotty Guy.

"You're a pretty funny-looking spotty kid," snorted the witch.

Meanwhile, Mr Valdini had dropped to his knees behind the counter and was crawling gingerly towards his phone. "999," he croaked. "I've got a witch in my cafe who's kidnapped twenty kids from the hospital."

"Oh yes?" said the desk sergeant, who was used to daft calls, "and we've got Margaret Thatcher doing a tap dance on the top of our table."

The police were in the middle of an important game of cards, but of course they had to check out complaints. They nearly fell out of their trousers when they found out it was true.

"We'll have to read you your rights, Ma'am," they said to the witch.

"That's kind," said the witch. "For one horrible moment I thought you were going to read me my wrongs."

The police took off their helmets and scratched their heads, the way policemen do when they're trying to get their brains to work.

"We're taking these kids back to hospital," they said, "and you'll have to go to prison."

The witch, who didn't know how to cry, quickly splashed some lemonade on her face and wailed, "Oh

no! Not that! I'm only a poor old woman. My mother and father died yesterday. My house got burnt down in a riot. And I'm getting smallpox tomorrow – the hospital have jus' told me."

The police thought about their prison, and how full it was already with trouble makers. The witch looked as if she might turn out to be worse than the whole lot put together.

".O.K." they said, "but push off, Grandma."

As the children were driven off, waving, and thanking her for a great day out, the witch waved George like a flag and yelled, "The witch rules, O.K.!"

The Ace Baby-sitters

Simon drove home in an ambulance and his mother made a big fuss of him. But best of all, he didn't have to go back to school at the beginning of term. That was specially good because there was a new headmaster called Mr Lurnum.

"He's like a mad bull in a thunderstorm!" Jimmy Watson told Simon. "He even ticks Sally off!"

Meanwhile, Simon enjoyed himself. He limped dramatically round the house – making sure his mother didn't think he was getting better again too quickly; and he was allowed to play with clay on the kitchen table. But after a week or two of such bliss, he began to grow bored and when his mother said she was going out for the evening, he wanted to go with her.

"I don't think so," his mother said. "I wonder if that old woman friend of yours would baby-sit?"

"D'you mean the witch!?" gasped Simon.

"She'll hear you calling her that one day," his mother warned. "I think I'll write to her."

The witch was astonished; a bit shocked; and very pleased. She wrote back:

Dear Mrs Woman,

I didnt no yoo HAD any babees.
I certunly dont think I shud sit on it
if yoo did. A skwoshed babee wud be no
yoose to anyone. But I'll cum and play with Simon.
O. K?

She stuffed a large bag full of things she thought might amuse him, including her book of magic spells, a wand – and George of course. Simon's mother could see the witch struggling up the path. She felt slightly alarmed, but it was too late to change her mind. She let the witch in and told her, "You'll find everything you need."

"Will I?" said the witch.

"And Simon goes to bed at nine o'clock."

"Does he?" said the witch.

"And I should be back about ten."

"Should you?" said the witch.

Simon's mother felt slightly alarmed again but hurried off.

"We can play with clay in the kitchen," Simon said.

"I think I'll have a bath first," the witch announced. "Your mother said I could."

Simon looked surprised.

"I hope you've got plenty of yellow ducks in your bathroom."

"Only a plastic boat," apologised Simon.

"That will have to do," snorted the witch, trying unsuccessfully to hide her disappointment.

She flung off most of her clothes and leapt into the bath. There was a huge wave which landed on the floor and turned the bathmat into a kind of raft. Simon watched anxiously as blobs of water trickled through the kitchen ceiling. He wished she'd hurry up, but the witch had dumped George into the plastic boat and was busy whizzing him up and down the bath. When the bath was so full of black hairs that not even the witch could stand it, she came downstairs.

"Now shall we play with the clay?" Simon said.

"I feel like having visitors," said the witch. "Can I use your phone? Your mother said I could."

The witch had a lot of relations. They were witches like herself, and she rang them all. "Bring spell books," she yelled.

There was a whirring noise in the air as half a dozen witches arrived on their broomsticks and landed with a flump in the garden.

"Is this the wee boy?" asked Hatty The Howl, " – the skinny one with the broken leg?"

"This is Simon," said the witch. "His mother told me to keep him amused."

The witches gaggled indoors. There was Winnie from Wapping, Awful Aggie, Daring Doreen, Frances the Frightful, and Molly the Moan.

"Hullo, Simon the Sickly," they greeted.

Simon was both aghast and delighted.

"There's clay in the kitchen," he told them. "We're allowed to make a mess."

"ALLOWED TO MAKE A MESS!" whooped all the witches. "Now where shall we begin?"

"With a competition," grinned the witch. "Spellbooks allowed."

Awful Aggie flung her spell book open at page one and wagged a boney finger down it.

"Pease and pods and treacly puddings
pop into a pan," she said.

The fridge door blew off, a bag of frozen peas jumped into a pan, turned into a treacle pudding which boiled furiously and then exploded like a firework and stuck itself to the ceiling.

"Not bad," said the witch.

Simon looked worried.

Frightful Frances read out,

"Humpty Dumptys, sitting on a wall,
All topple over and have a great fall."

Simon's mother's free range eggs did a highland fling along the shelf and then flung themselves, one by one, onto the floor shouting, "Hoots mon! Scotland forever!"

All the witches rolled around laughing.

"They must have been Scotch eggs!" hooted the witch. "Very funny, Fanny."

Daring Doreen looked peeved. She'd been going to do that trick. She pinched Frances's bottom and blamed it on her cat.

"I'm better now," gasped Simon. "I don't need no more amusing."

"Course you do, darling," said Hatty. "You look green."

Daring Doreen was still scowling into her spell book. "I'll jump off the roof," she said, "and I'll turn myself into a seagull on the way down."

"Oh jolly good," giggled the witches, plodding out into the garden and making themselves comfortable on the lawn to watch.

It was dark, and daring Doreen had trouble feeling where the house had gone, let alone the roof.

"I can see her!" howled Awful Aggie. "She's hanging onto the chimney."

Daring Doreen was having more trouble reading her spell book. She twisted it round under the light of the moon and decided it said,

"Oh man in the moon and sooty night,
Like a screaming gull I'm gonna take flight."

Then she galloped along the top of the roof and took off into space. The witches expected to see a woofting white seagull. It didn't happen.

"She looks more like a bat to me," snorted Winnie from Wapping, "and she's coming too fast to be flying."

"She's just ordinary old falling," scoffed Aggie.

Daring Doreen had just landed. There was an awful silence which seemed to go on forever, and then a lot of bad language and Doreen shouting, "What a bloomin' stupid place to put a rose bush!"

"Foul!" declared the witch. "No points."

"No points!" screamed Doreen, pulling prickles out of her knickers. The rose bush was a wreck. It had not been trained to withstand the weight of falling witches.

"My mother will . . . ," started Simon.

"I never had a mother," wailed Molly the Moan.

"*Everybody's* had a mother," scoffed Hatty.

"Not me," moaned Molly. "I was found under a gooseberry bush."

The other witches tried not to laugh.

"Get your spell book out and cheer up," said Winnie.

The writing in Molly the Moan's spell book was all smudged where Molly had dripped tears on it.

"My tricks are boring," moaned Molly.

"You can say that again," groaned the witch.

"My tricks are boring," moaned Molly again. "I'll just turn the beans into worms," she sighed.

"All right then, Ducky," said Hatty, "so get on with it."

Molly waved her hand wearily and the runner beans turned into worms; wriggled for a few seconds, and fell down dead.

"How typical," said the witch.

Simon wished all the spells were as untroublesome as that, but Molly the Moan locked herself in the bathroom and filled the bath with tears. Another horrible damp patch appeared on the ceiling.

Several front doors in the road were beginning to

open and Simon could see the neighbours peering about.

"You'd better all come back inside," he whispered.

"Yes, it's gruesome out here," agreed Winnie, "and I can't read my spell book in the dark. Look what happened to Doreen's seagull trick!"

Giggling and shoving, the witches flopped across the lawn like a lot of moth-eaten crows.

"Is there a prize for this competition by the way?" asked Winnie.

"Course there is," said the witch.

"I'm feeling *much* better now," said Simon. "You needn't bother doing any more."

"It's no bother," said Winnie. "For you, little hop along, I'll do one of my very best spells."

Whilst Winnie from Wapping was thinking, the witch fried some sausages and dipped them in marmalade. Everyone agreed they were delicious.

"Right," said Winnie, sticking her unfinished sausage under a cushion. "This one will win the competition. Listen to this,

> Little Bo Peep has lost her sheep
> And doesn't know where to find them.
> Go up the stairs and open the drawers
> And there you will probably find them."

"You'd better not go up to my mother's bedroom," gasped Simon.

64

"Got to, my lovely," said Winnie, "that's where all the sheep are hiding." She pulled open the dressing table drawers and out jumped all Simon's mother's best jumpers. They had fluffy legs, and eyes and noses, and they pattered round the room saying, "Baa."

The leader of them suddenly sniffed fresh air and off they all shuffled through the front door on their way to the park.

"Gosh!" cried Simon in dismay. "What will my mother say?"

"She'll say we're very good babysitters I expect," laughed Winnie.

"It's my turn now," said Hatty the Howl. "All get on the beds, quickly."

"It can't be better than my trick," said Winnie.

"It'll be a lot more exciting," promised Hatty. She began to recite —

> "Round and round the bedrooms,
> Up and down the stairs,
> In a racing brum brum,
> Hold tight and say your prayers!"

Without warning, the beds shot off like racing cars with everyone hanging on and screaming.

"You've got to dodge us, not bash into us," yelled Hatty to Simon and the witches on the other beds.

"It's more fun bashing!" shrieked Awful Aggie.

She took a big chunk out of the wardrobe.

"Woman driver!" yelled Winnie from Wapping.

Awful Aggie bumped beds even harder and the plaster fell off the ceiling.

"I thought it looked like snow," moaned Molly.

"Let's skid down the mountain side," whooped Hatty the Howl.

The beds shot out of the bedrooms to the top of the stairs. They wobbled for a few seconds, and then raced down the staircase.

"Gosh! What fun!" gasped Hatty.

"My mother'll . . . ," choked Simon.

The witch, who had ears sharper than a bat's, could hear footsteps coming down the road. It was about ten o'clock.

"Time this boy was in bed," she said. "You lot can go home now."

"But who's won the competition?" asked the witches.

"Hatty has."

"And what's the prize?" howled Hatty.

"It's a knitted loo roll cover."

"Oh how useful," said Hatty, giving it away immediately to Molly the Moan and saying, "Happy Christmas".

"Leave by the back door," the witch was saying, "and don't leave any cats or spell books lying about."

Simon's mother was closing the garden gate and coming up the path. Hastily, the witch waved her magic wand over everything in sight and the whole place returned to normal.

"Oh," said the witch, rubbing her eyes sleepily as Simon's mother came in, "I was nearly dozing off."

"Where's Simon?" asked his mother.

"Sssssssssh, asleep for ages," whispered the witch.

Simon's mother looked pleased, and a little bit surprised. The house looked remarkably neat.

"I suppose you'd be offended if I offered you money," she said.

"No I wouldn't," said the witch.

She stuffed the money under her hat and shuffled off.

When Simon got up next morning he was astonished to see everywhere looking so tidy. Probably the bathroom was a mess, but it wasn't. Surely downstairs must be a wreck, but it wasn't either.

"Did you hear any bumps or bangs last night?" his mother asked him.

"Not specially," said Simon, carefully.

"No riots or civil disturbances?" his mother went on.

"I don't think so," said Simon, glancing cautiously out of the window to see if the garden was still there. " – Why?"

"Oh nothing," said his mother. "It's just something the neighbours were saying."

"I feel like going back to school," Simon said.

George Gets Hung

Simon did seem to have recovered remarkably quickly, and his mother agreed he could go back to school.

"It's safer here!" he explained to his friend, Jimmy Watson. "You should've seen what those witches did to our house!"

"D'you mean you know lots of other witches and not just *her*?"

"Oh yes," said Simon. "All her relations: and their bloomin' cats."

Jimmy Watson didn't know whether he believed Simon and decided he didn't. A bit humphed, Simon marched off to see the witch.

The witch's house was as big a mess as ever; small and shabby and almost completely hidden behind cabbages and nasturtiums which had gone berserk, strangling not only the railings but the bus stop as

69

well. The witch was almost completely hidden under a mass of twisted sellotape.

"Are you going to post yourself!?" giggled Simon. The witch had only half a nose left and no eyes at all.

"You look like a parcel," said Simon, beginning to un-peel her.

"I'm mending my spell book. Stupid boy!" snapped the witch, crossly. "I've already mislaid at least half a dozen good spells." She gave George a malicious stare.

George gave her one back, just as good, and washed a half-eaten spell about frogs and princes out of the fluff round his whiskers.

"I'll be dishonoured among witches if I lose any more," grumbled the witch, flicking over a few more tattered pages and complaining, "this lot here are dead old fashioned."

Simon could see that the witch was getting herself into a state so he said, "Surely spells never go out of date, do they?"

"D'you want Tuesday the seventh back again then?" snapped the witch. "Didn't you finish using it up before Wednesday came?"

Simon looked muddled. "I just meant, I *liked* the old sort of spells, like changing princes into frogs, and that sort of thing."

"Oh yes, you mean the one that flea ridden rag bag has just eaten do you?"

George continued to look unconcerned; the witch regularly forgot to feed him so he felt no sorrow about helping himself to the wrong things. The witch's grumbles were interrupted by a loud howling noise coming up her footpath. Then the doorbell rang.

The witch didn't feel like visitors at that moment – her spell book being all in a muddle and only rubbishy tricks left in it. She was even more put out when she discovered the visitor was Hatty the Howl, looking disgustingly healthy and organised.

"Dear heart!" greeted Hatty, tossing her pointed hat onto the hat stand which promptly collapsed because George had eaten the screws for lunch. "Long time no see!"

"It was only last week," muttered the witch. "Are you stopping?"

But Hatty the Howl was already sitting down in the comfy sort of way visitors sit when they are going to stay a long time.

"And what's this, oh cunning cousin?" she howled, waving her elegant black nails at the dilapidated spell book.

"What does it look like?" sulked the witch.

"A bit of a mess?" suggested Hatty.

"You can't judge a book by its cover," the witch snapped.

"But it hasn't *got* a cover!" chortled Hatty.

Simon could see danger glinting in the witch's

eyes. Hatty the Howl was well known for her super dramatic spells and he knew the witch would be bursting to show off. Which she was.

"I can do anything YOU can!" she scoffed.

"Oh I *believe* you, darling ducky – so change that scruffy cat of yours into something better. Lord knows the poor thing could do with a change."

Panicking quietly, the witch thumbed through the spell book. Blobs of soup covered up the important words, and bits and pieces of squashed spiders made small words into long ones.

"Can't you decide?" tittered Hatty.

"Decent spells can't be hurried," snapped the witch. She had decided to turn George into a black panther. If the panther looked ferocious enough, it might make Hatty leave early.

She looked up 'changes', and 'p' for panther. Unfortunately a piece of spaghetti shaped like an orange worm was stuck over part of the spell, but Hatty was getting impatient so the witch hurriedly garbled the magic words and stabbed her wand with a swoosh at George. Strange things began to happen to the cat. His fluff started to twitch and stiffen. Then his body turned flat and square, and with an indignant meiow, George changed into a picture in a fancy frame. The witch was aghast.

"Sweetheart!" Hatty exclaimed, "that was most awfully clever!"

"I know," said the witch, dumping the picture of George on the mantlepiece and wondering what on earth had gone wrong with the rotten old spell. However, Hatty the Howl seemed so impressed with the trick, the witch invited her to stay for tea and made sausage and earwigs on toast. George stared blankly down at the feast.

"Well, that was marvellous," said Hatty, wiping her mouth politely on the hem of her dress and belching appreciatively. "I'd better fly – aren't you going to change that cat back again?"

"Not yet," said the witch. "He's more convenient up there. I can hoover up some of his mangy fur whilst he's out of the way."

"Good idea," agreed Hatty, promptly vanishing.

Simon went too. His mother had been making scones when he'd left and he never felt like eating in the witch's house.

A week later he went back to see the witch. She was sitting with her chin in her hands, scowling dismally at the mantlepiece. Then Simon saw that George was still propped up in his frame.

"Good heavens!" he exclaimed. "Haven't you changed him back again yet?"

"Can't," said the witch. "What d'you think I've been trying to do all week. See there – ", she flung the spell book at Simon, "it goes from page forty one to page forty three. It serves that wretched animal right if he's gone and eaten up the change-back-again answer. He's gone and framed himself!"

"But if you think really hard, don't you think you could remember the backwards spell?"

"No," spat the witch, "and anyway, he's less of a bloomin' nuisance up there."

But secretly, she knew that a witch without a cat was as disgraceful as a pudding without a basin.

"Go through the whole book," suggested Simon, "you're bound to find something that works."

"It's no use," said the witch. "I *know* it was on page forty two and that stupid cat . . . picture up there's eaten it."

"Take the picture to the vet," said Simon, feebly.

"Any more brilliant ideas like that?" scoffed the witch.

"Well . . . take it to a . . ."

"Yes? dot dot dot?"

"A, er, picture man: he might sort of discover something funny about it," said Simon, even more feebly.

"Well I'm sick of it hanging round here anyway," said the witch, and threw George into her shopping trolley.

There was an antique shop in the high street. It sold everything from plastic egg cups to diamond tiaras. There were also stacks of mouldy looking pictures hanging about.

"Just the very place," said Simon.

There was a bouncy bell on the back of the door and an old man with spectacles answered it.

"Yes, can I help you Madam?"

"Mebbe," muttered the witch, "you can look at this picture and see if you can see a cat in it?"

"Well of course I can see a cat in it," said the antique dealer, taking off his spectacles so he could see it better. "Good heavens!" he exclaimed, getting suddenly very excited, "do you know what you've got here?!"

The witch shrugged and said, "you tell me, old fuddy duddy."

"This is a genuine GROTTY!"

"A genuine wotty?" asked the witch, whispering behind her hand to Simon, "the old dunce is barmy!"

"This cat has been painted by the famous Grotty," the old man gibbered on, "oh my goodness, what a find! Where did you get it?"

"S'been hanging around my house hundreds of years, that cat has," said the witch truthfully.

"It's for sale I hope?" the antique dealer said.

This was something the witch hadn't considered. A cunning look crossed her face. She'd never got much change out of George. Rather, he was a fearful expense in ruined furniture and half-eaten rugs. The only item of furniture he *hadn't* eaten was the television – and that was only because he liked *Coronation Street*.

"You wouldn't, would you?" gasped Simon, shocked.

"Shut up!" said the witch. "How much?"

"A hundred pounds," said the antique dealer.

The witch choked.

"Two hundred then," the old man corrected.

The witch choked again.

"I've offended you," the dealer apologised, "—five hundred?"

"Done!" the witch managed to croak.

"I think that's *awful*," said Simon as they walked away.

"Who asked your opinion?" said the witch.

"But now you've got no cat at all," complained Simon.

"So what," replied the witch. "I could buy five HUNDRED cats with all this money."

"They wouldn't be the same as George though."

"That could only be a mercy," retorted the witch, and shot off.

Simon went home and didn't eat his tea or his supper so his mother decided he was ill and put him to bed early. In the morning he told her what the witch had done, but all his mother said was, "Darling, you mustn't make up such stories. Cats don't turn into pictures, and just because that poor old lady is a bit strange looking, you shouldn't call her a witch."

But Simon went on worrying, and when school was over he went to look in the antique shop. The picture of George was in the window now and it had a ticket on it which said a thousand pounds. Simon whistled in amazement. He was still standing with his mouth open when Lady Fox-Custard appeared. Lady Fox-Custard lived in the biggest house in the village. In fact, everything she had was the biggest and the grandest, (the witch was her biggest enemy). Not many people liked Fox-Custard but they pretended like mad that they did. The mayor pretended, and the vicar pretended, and the headmaster pretended. She was that sort of woman.

It so happened that she was having a bridge party and she always liked to have something new and posh on show when the visitors came, sticking out in a place where they couldn't possibly fail to notice it.

"I want something EXQUISITE," she boomed at the antique dealer.

"Of course M'Lady," bowed the dealer, pretending.

"Pretty expensive you understand."

"I understand perfectly," creepy crawlied the old man. "I have just the thing for you – only came in the other day. A real snip at only a thousand pounds." He showed her the picture of George.

Lady Fox-Custard shuddered. It reminded her of something horrible but she couldn't think what.

"It's a genuine Grotty," the old man went on. "You won't find another like it."

Lady Fox-Custard hoped she jolly well wouldn't.

"Genuine, did you say?"

"As yourself," said the old man.

So Lady Fox-Custard handed over the thousand pounds and put George on a genuine gold plastic table in her drawing room.

When Simon told the witch what had happened, she was livid.

"I'm not standing for THAT!" she screeched.

She grabbed her handbag, stuffing into it whatever she could think of; a rubber mouse, a pair of binoculars, the remains of her lunch and swept off in the mood for battle.

The bridge party was in full swing, and Lady Fox-Custard was dealing the playing cards at high speed and rattling her diamond rings. The vicar, the mayor, and Mr Lurnum were quite blinded by so much flashing but passed no remark.

"One spade," blinked the vicar.

"Two no trumps," said the mayor.

Mr Lurnum couldn't concentrate: there was a picture crowding him off his chair and a stiff looking cat glaring at him. It looked horribly familiar.

"That's a real Grotty," explained Lady Fox-Custard.

"Oh, I wouldn't say that," said the vicar, who was

a polite man and had never been known to say anything nastier than 'bother'.

Lady Fox-Custard gave him a scornful look.

"Three hearts," said the mayor, trying to get on with the game.

"I bought it from a little man in the High Street," Lady Fox-Custard struggled on. "Frightfully expensive of course, but then, in MY position, one must have decentish sorts of things."

"Of course," agreed the vicar.

The witch had arrived at the window. She was standing on a prize marrow and peering through the glass with a pair of binoculars.

"Eeeh!" exclaimed Simon, "that marrow – she'll murder you!"

But the witch only had eyes for George. How DARE that custard tart kidnap her cat. She eased the window up with the tip of her nose.

"Here, kitty kitty," she hissed.

Lady Fox-Custard fancied she heard something horrible and hissy, but carried on playing.

The witch nosed the window up higher and flung the rubber mouse at George. It hit him on the nose and bounced onto the middle of the card table.

"Lor' sakes!" screeched Lady Fox-Custard. "What on h'earth's going on 'ere!?"

"Something is!" said Mr Lurnum, darkly.

"Most extraordinary!" agreed the vicar.

"That stupid dumb cat!" yelled the witch, jumping up and down on the marrow until it was pulped into a jammy mess of nothing.

"Eeeh?" said Simon again, looking around nervously for the gardener.

The witch only had the remains of her lunch left with which to tempt George away from Lady Fox-Custard's mansion, and Simon didn't understand how she expected George to behave when he was still only a painted picture of himself.

But aiming viciously, the witch hurled the half-eaten sandwich in George's direction. This time, she hit the little table on which he was displayed and the whole thing, including the picture collapsed onto the floor.

"Oh my Grotty!" screamed Lady Fox-Custard.

"It's torn!" gasped the vicar.

"And so expensive it was," the mayor said, trying not to titter.

And at that moment, Lady Fox-Custard spotted the witch. "I might have known!" she exclaimed. "Rubber mice, beetle sandwiches, and childish tricks! And vandalising me mansion as well!"

But the vicar was staring in disbelief at the broken picture. A furry paw was feeling around the edges of the frame, and then George's whiskers began to twitch. A second paw appeared, and a lot of dusty fluff, and finally a black mangy body squeezed out onto the carpet.

"It's m'Boy!" cried the witch, emotionally, "come to me, beloved cat!"

But George, now fully recovered, slithered across the room and then bolted through the window.

"Never mind," muttered the witch, "he'll have gone straight home. Brainless animal!"

As Simon and the witch hurried after him, they could hear Lady Fox-Custard shouting about theft, and breaking and entering, and fraud, and getting the police.

"She'll never prove it, that mouldy old custard," giggled the witch. "Imagine her standing up in court and saying, 'this picture what I've got, jumped off a table, turned into a real cat, and ran away – yer 'onour'. They'd lock her up!"

Meanwhile George had arrived home and eaten up the witch's wand. He wasn't having the wretched thing waved at him again.

The Witch's Firework

The term wore on slowly and nothing much happened, mainly because George had eaten the witch's wand. The witch had sent away for a new one, but it was a long time coming.

"I *nearly* feel like breaking another leg," Simon grumbled.

Mr Lurnum was on the platform and he was doing his impression of a mad bull. The children, who had grown used to his booming voice, were just about properly asleep when they heard the word 'fireworks'.

". . . they're very dangerous, and they're HIDEOUSLY expensive," Mr Lurnum was saying. "So, first of all, we're having 'em here, and secondly, we've got to raise money to buy 'em."

"I'm sick of bringing money in to school," whispered Sally.

Mr Lurnum got off the stage and boomed into Sally's ear, "Nobody's asking you for your pocket money, little Miss Clever Cloggs, I'm running a school disco."

Simon couldn't imagine his mother wanting to come to a disco, and Jimmy Watson said that his father would rather do a month in the salt mines. Lady Fox-Custard thought it was a perfectly wonderful idea and looked forward to wearing a new dress.

"Have we all got to dress up?" the witch asked Simon.

"The boys don't, but the ladies usually do," said Simon. "You don't need to bother coming at all really," he added, nervously.

"S'no bother," said the witch. "I've never been to a disco before."

There was a shop in the high street which had the sort of clothes the witch liked. It was called Oxfam.

"Gimme a ball gown," she said to the ladies serving.

The Oxfam ladies looked the witch up and down and said, "Wouldn't you rather buy a nice warm skirt and a woolly cardigan, dear?"

"No I wouldn't!" snapped the witch. "I'm going to a disco, not a grannies' tea party."

As it happened, Lady Fox-Custard had been getting rid of a pile of clothes. They were so old, even the moths had brought up their young in them and moved on to newer nesting places.

"That's a nice one," said the witch, pulling out a very shiny dress dotted with diamanté and squeezing herself into it.

The Oxfam ladies didn't like to tell the witch she looked terrible in the dress, so they let her have it for 5p.

Everybody turned up for the disco, because no one wanted to get into Mr Lurnum's bad books. The witch was astonished at the noise.

"Won't the police come?!" she gasped.

"It's disco music," laughed Simon.

"It sounds like a riot," the witch said.

"I'd rather be in a riot," Mr Watson grumbled.

Just then, Lady Fox-Custard swept in. She was wearing a new pink dress which looked like a squashed blancmange. She hated the noise of the disco music but wanted to show off her dress and look young and beautiful, so she treacled up to Mr Lurnum and squeaked, "What a wunnerful little disco! . . . boo boopy doop!"

"Gosh!" groaned Sally, "she's not even in the right century! What an embarrassing woman."

Lady Fox-Custard heard and went pink. Then she saw her black diamanté dress on the witch and went purple. The witch was in the middle of the hall, body popping. Her bust, and her tummy, and her bottom, were like three rubber tyres, all popping in different

directions. Everybody *knew* that she was wearing one of Lady Fox-Custard's old dresses, and was making it look unbelievably awful.

"Wouldn't you think that stupid woman would wear something her own size!" snooted Lady Fox-Custard.

"And it's such a common-looking dress," said Mr Watson.

All this time, George had been trying to get in, but Mr Lurnum, who was selling tickets at the door, wouldn't let him. George started making horrible noises. Even more horrible than the disco music.

"Sir won't let your cat in," shouted Simon at the witch, "and your cat's taken umbrage."

"The thievin' little varmint!" snapped the witch. "He's always taking something he shouldn't."

She shot to the door and found George licking out the inside of an empty chip carton.

"Put that umbrage back where you found it, you thievin' moggy," she yelled at him.

George stared at the witch coldly and put the chip carton back in the litter bin, then he shot through her legs into the disco. He fancied dancing with Lady Fox-Custard and whizzed round her in black circles, but accidentally caught his claws in her new dress. Lady Fox-Custard screamed hysterically and went straight home.

"Trust that bad woman friend of yours to ruin everything," Sally said to Simon.

Next day, Mr Lurnum was annoyed to find that the disco hadn't made as much money as he'd hoped. He was specially anxious to have a good firework night because he wanted the mayor, and the vicar, and the Oxfam ladies, and the school inspector to see him doing something sparkley and think what a good headmaster he was.

"We'll have to think of something else," he grumbled, "or Guy Fawkes night is going to turn out a damp squib."

At playtime, the children ganged together and decided to get the rest of the money themselves.

"We'll make guys," said one of the boys, "and we're bound to collect enough money by the end of the week."

Jimmy Watson was madly excited when his mother said that the pyjamas he'd been wearing were finished with and that he could use them for his guy. He stuffed them with newspaper, used a burst football for the head, onto which he painted a hideous face, and topped the lot with his sister's wig. Simon agreed it was a fantastic guy.

"My mother won't let me use *anything*," he complained. "I've got loads of nasty looking jumpers but she keeps telling me they're good enough for school. I feel like a guy in them, but she says clothes are too expensive to waste."

Jimmy Watson said that mothers were weird, but

he was too delighted with his own guy to keep a sorry face on himself for long. The whole town seemed to be crammed full of guys. People were hard put to dodge them.

"Personally, I think it's pretty disgusting," said Sally's mother. "Nothing short of begging. That's what I say."

But nobody wanted to hear what Sally's mother had to say.

"Bet she turns up for the firework night, though," said another mother.

Meanwhile, Simon was guy-less. Despondent, he wandered down to the town. He cheered up when he happened to bump into the witch. She was hurrying out of the chemist's, looking very pleased with herself.

"I've bought some super lipstick, and some eyeshadow," she told Simon.

"YOU?!" exclaimed Simon.

"Why not?" the witch frowned. "I can look nice if I want to, can't I? I'm not too old, am I? Or too ugly? I'm as good as anyone else, aren't I?"

Simon realised he'd made a mistake and said hurriedly that it was because he thought she didn't *need* make-up.

"Oh very cunning!" snorted the witch, "but I'll treat you to a coffee and a cream bun if you're good."

It was only when they sat down in the cafe that

Simon noticed the witch was still wearing her disco dress. Then to his embarrassment, she got out the lipstick and painted it generously onto her mouth, smudging it somewhat so that she looked as if she was eating a giant poppy. The eyeshadow she'd chosen was brilliant pink with glitzy bits in it. The witch put plenty of that on too.

"Yes?" said the waitress, slowly pouring some cups sideways off a tray because she was so busy gawping at the witch.

"Two coffees and two cream buns," said the witch.

"Two coffees and two beam cruns," said the waitress, walking away backwards and knocking customers over as she went.

After six cream buns, the witch's lipstick had spread even further. Then Simon spotted Mrs Watson, zig zagging through the tables, her open handbag clutched in her hand.

"Simon!" she cried, "how CLEVER of you! That's got to be the best guy in town. You must have been up all night." And she gave him twenty pence.

Horrified, Simon realized that Mrs Watson thought that the witch wasn't real, but a guy which he himself had made. But to his amazement, the witch seemed flattered and was cackling with pleasure.

"We're on to a good thing here, eh, lad? Good thing, what!" she dug her boney elbows into Simon's ribs. "Let's go before me make-up gets spoilt."

"The best place to sit is outside the post office," she said, "so's we'll catch everyone coming out with their pensions and their dole money." And ignoring Simon's shocked expression, she plonked herself down on the pavement with her legs stretched out across the post office doorway. Simon felt positively consternated as the needy and the aged tripped over the witch, one after another. But, astonishingly, nearly everyone threw money into the witch's hat, which she had jammed between her knees.

"What a guy," they said. Or "That's a good un," or "You'd swear it was alive!"

By the end of the day Simon and the witch had a whole pile of money, and the witch was saying that she was thinking of going into films, or on the telly, perhaps.

Mr Lurnum, who had been pretending not to know that half his school was out and about, begging, accepted all the money with a grunt and hurried off to buy the fireworks before anyone (such as Sally's mother) could object. As soon as it grew dark, the children and their parents turned up at the school.

Sally's mother arrived and stood between the mayor and the vicar.

"I do so think these functions are worth supporting," she said.

"Yes indeed," said the mayor and the vicar.

The witch's new magic wand had arrived in that morning's post, and she wiggled it briefly at Sally's mother's legs. Astonished, Sally watched her mother sink six inches into the ground, her new high heels hidden under the mud.

It was the best Guy Fawkes' night the children had ever been to. It was so BIG. They all agreed it was much better than having to dash from one friend's garden to another and getting into trouble for various things, like tramping on parents' best plants etcetera.

"That's it," Mr Lurnum was saying. "I hope you enjoyed my firework display."

"HIS firework display!" sniffed Jimmy Watson. "All he did was to go out and buy them."

"Just a minute," the witch was saying. "Just one little mo'. I've got a firework of my own to light."

"Well hurry up, old lady," said Mr Lurnum, irritably.

"Oh no," complained Sally's mother, "her miserable little firework will make a poor ending to a lovely night."

With her tongue carefully poked out, the witch lit the blue touch paper, using the end of her new magic wand as a lighter. There was a wonderful swoosh and a thousand and one pink stars shot into the sky. They lit up the whole town and went on and on twinkling brilliantly.

"Oh look!" cried everyone in amazement, "they spell something."

In giant letters the firework said,

The witch shuffled off, grinning hugely.

"I'm going to leave it up there all night," she said to Simon.